MOMMY, THERE'S A DINOSA IN THE CORNFIELD!

Written by: Diana LeGere
Illustrated by: Gustyawan

Gracelyn Books
Chesterfield, VA

Mommy, There's a Dinosaur in the Cornfield!

Published by Gracelyn Books
An imprint of Arabelle Publishing
Chesterfield, Virginia

Illustrated by: Gustyawan
Cover Design by: Narubi
Interior Design by: Aalishaa

Library of Congress Control Number: 2022949711
Printed in the United States of America, 2022
ISBN: 979-8-9562362-4-7

For Renee, who first inspired me to write years ago.
I hope you'll enjoy reading this story to Sawyer and Hudson
as much as I enjoyed reading it to you. I love you.

Cooper woke up before sunrise. It was the first day of summer break, and he couldn't sleep. Cooper had plans.

Every morning during the school year, he bathed, dressed, ate breakfast, brushed his teeth, and rode the bus to school. Today, he wasn't doing any of that. There would be no books, no homework, and no teachers. Nope. Cooper had plans.

He hopped out of bed and plunked his bare feet on the hardwood floor. Then, without taking a bath, getting dressed, or brushing his teeth, he walked out of his room and slammed the door shut. BANG! He marched down the hall, down the stairs, and headed toward the kitchen, where he knew his mother would be. She would not want him going outside barefoot in the dark, but he didn't care. Cooper had plans.

Cooper's curly red hair tumbled as he rushed toward the door. Without saying a word, he strolled right past his mother, bare feet and all, and out the back door. BANG!

"Cooper! Where are you going in the dark?
And where are your SHOES?" his mother
shouted. He didn't answer.

BUTTER

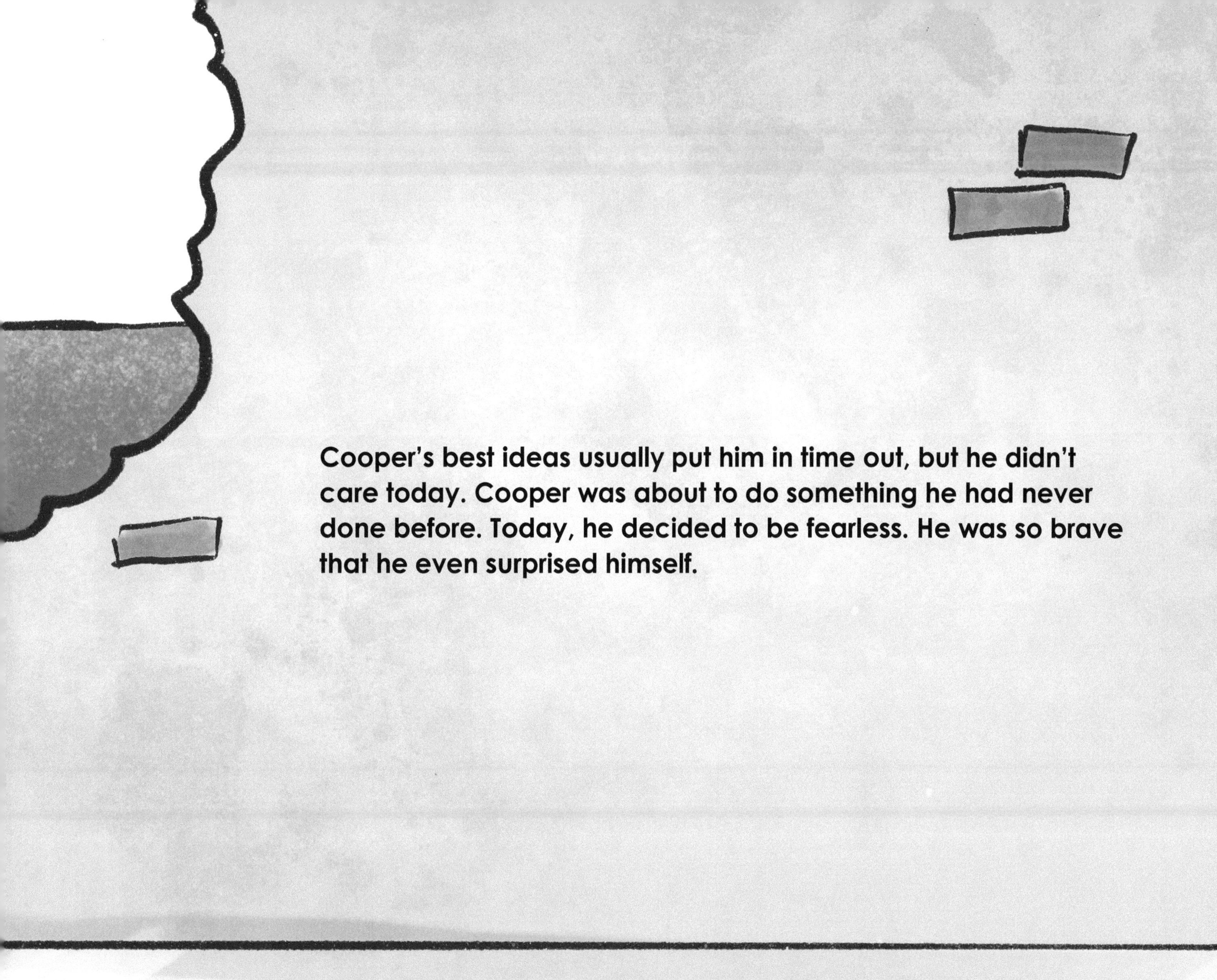

Cooper's best ideas usually put him in time out, but he didn't care today. Cooper was about to do something he had never done before. Today, he decided to be fearless. He was so brave that he even surprised himself.

Cooper ran to the giant oak tree in the yard and climbed the ladder to his tree house. This was Cooper's idea factory. Making wonderful plans was what he did best in this space. It was loaded with things that made thinking extra fun.

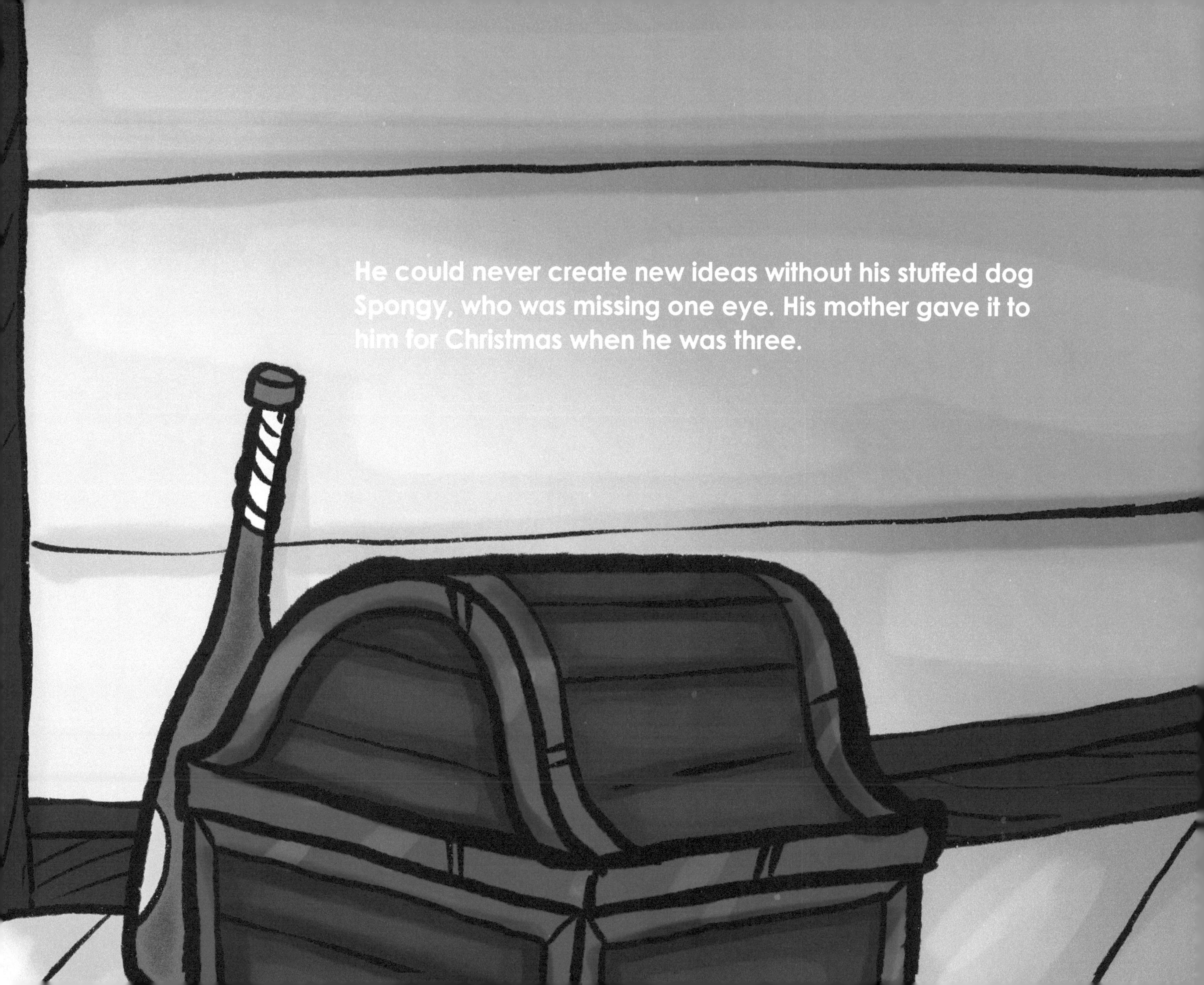

He could never create new ideas without his stuffed dog Spongy, who was missing one eye. His mother gave it to him for Christmas when he was three.

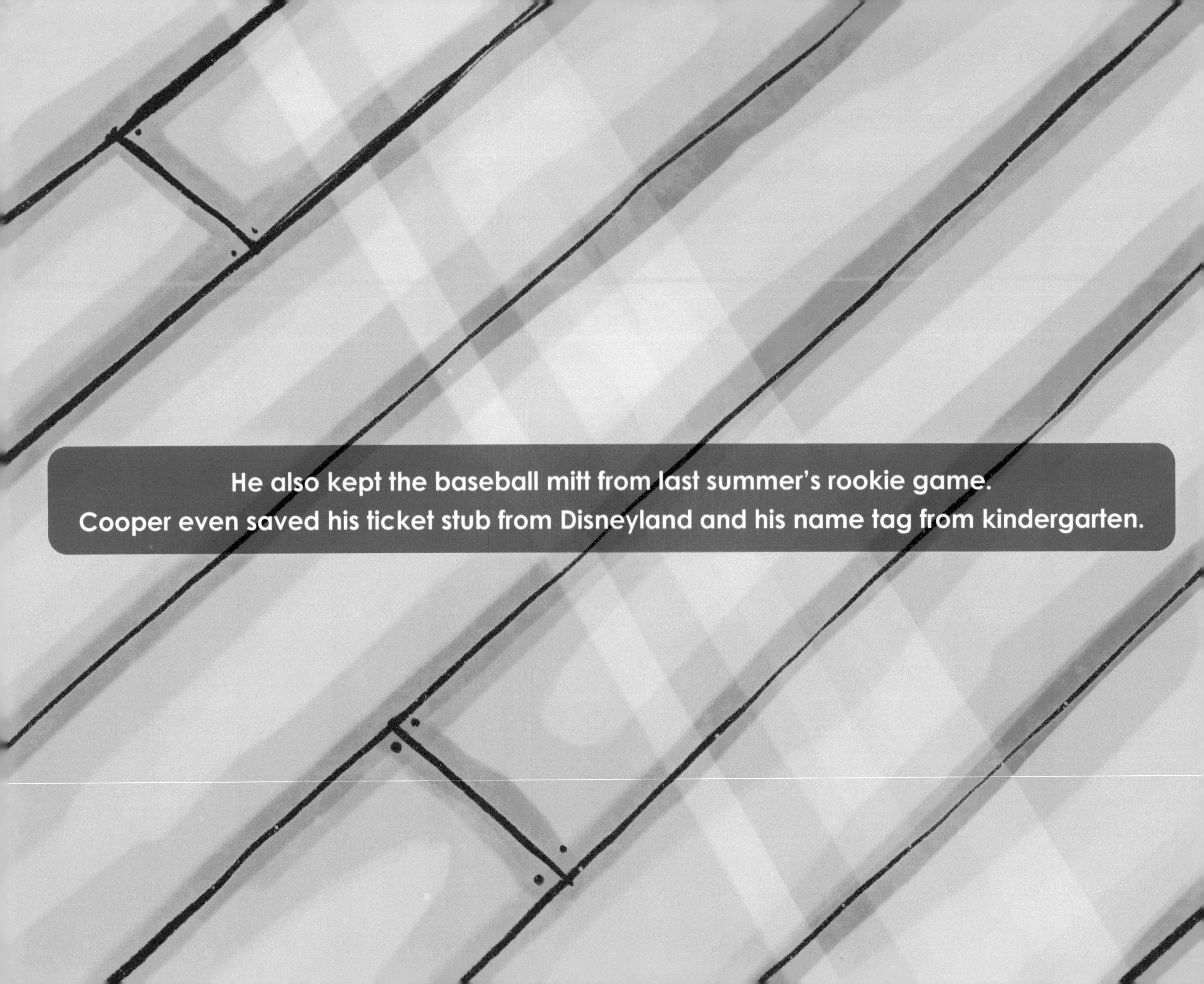

He also kept the baseball mitt from last summer's rookie game.
Cooper even saved his ticket stub from Disneyland and his name tag from kindergarten.

My name is
Cooper
TICKET
TICKET

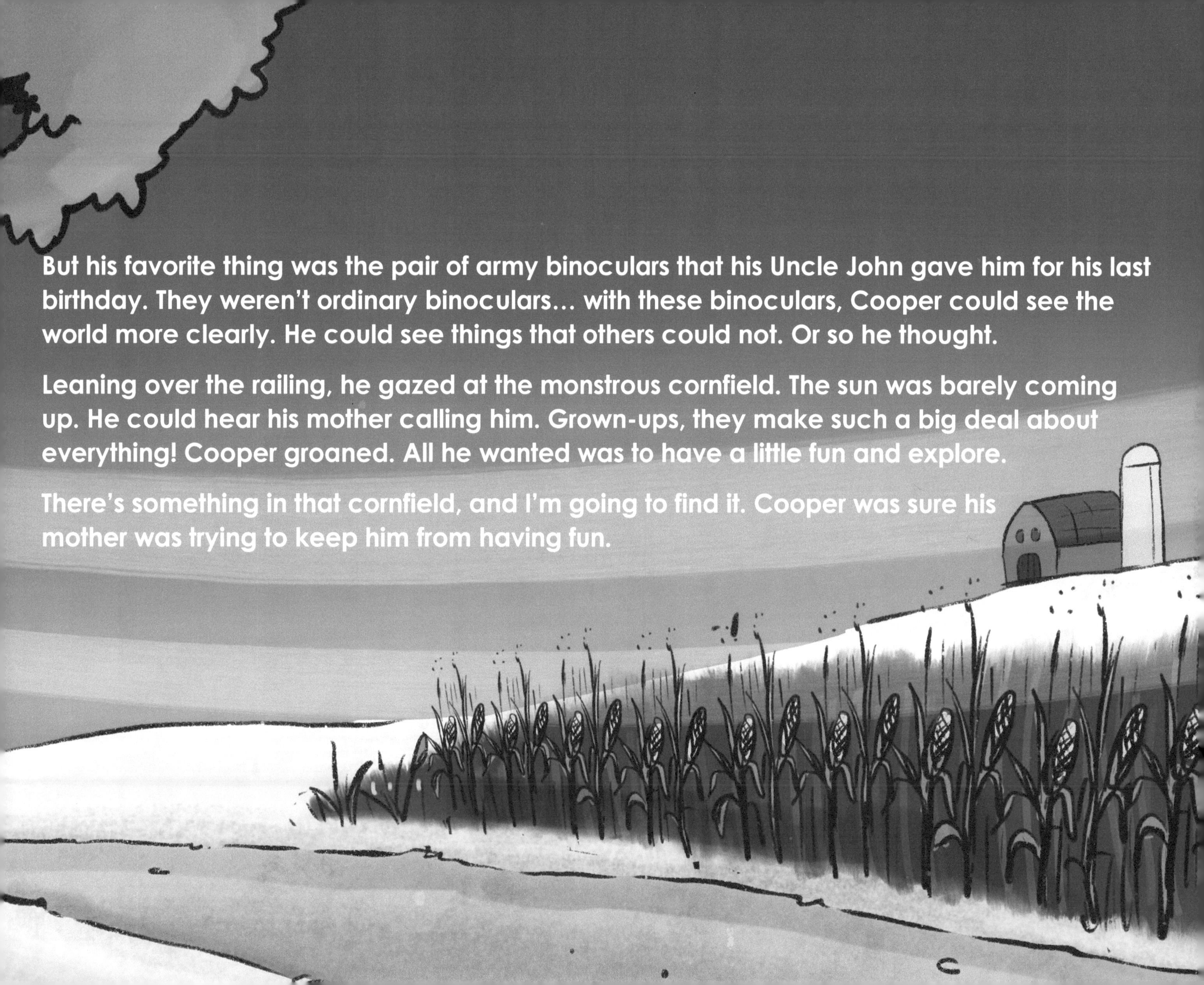

But his favorite thing was the pair of army binoculars that his Uncle John gave him for his last birthday. They weren't ordinary binoculars... with these binoculars, Cooper could see the world more clearly. He could see things that others could not. Or so he thought.

Leaning over the railing, he gazed at the monstrous cornfield. The sun was barely coming up. He could hear his mother calling him. Grown-ups, they make such a big deal about everything! Cooper groaned. All he wanted was to have a little fun and explore.

There's something in that cornfield, and I'm going to find it. Cooper was sure his mother was trying to keep him from having fun.

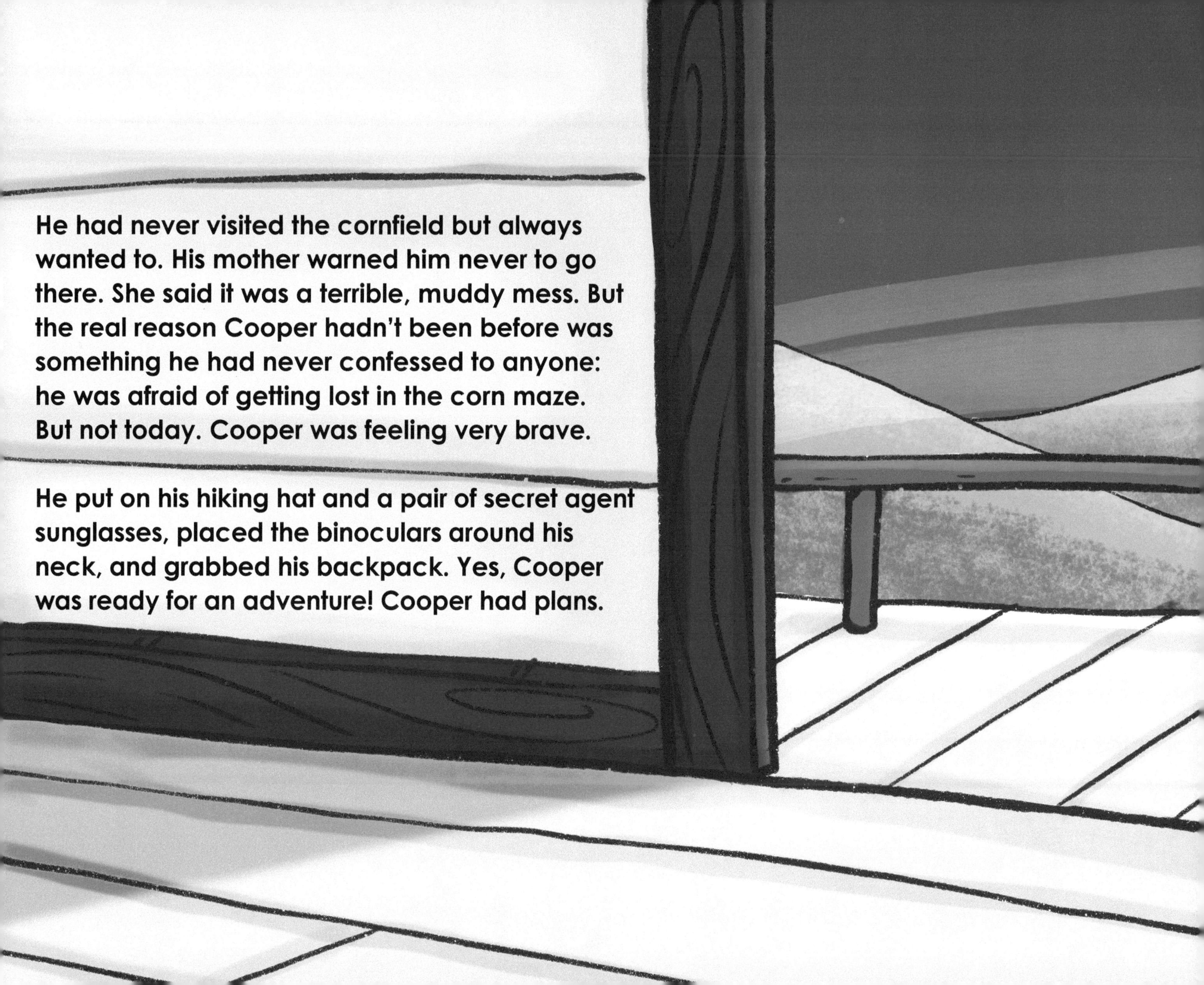

He had never visited the cornfield but always wanted to. His mother warned him never to go there. She said it was a terrible, muddy mess. But the real reason Cooper hadn't been before was something he had never confessed to anyone: he was afraid of getting lost in the corn maze. But not today. Cooper was feeling very brave.

He put on his hiking hat and a pair of secret agent sunglasses, placed the binoculars around his neck, and grabbed his backpack. Yes, Cooper was ready for an adventure! Cooper had plans.

He knew he had to move fast because being brave only lasts for a little while when you're six. He had to get to the cornfield before his mother found him. She was superb at sniffing out fun and wrecking it.

Like a brave soldier dressed for battle, Cooper climbed down the ladder and marched straight into the cornfield.

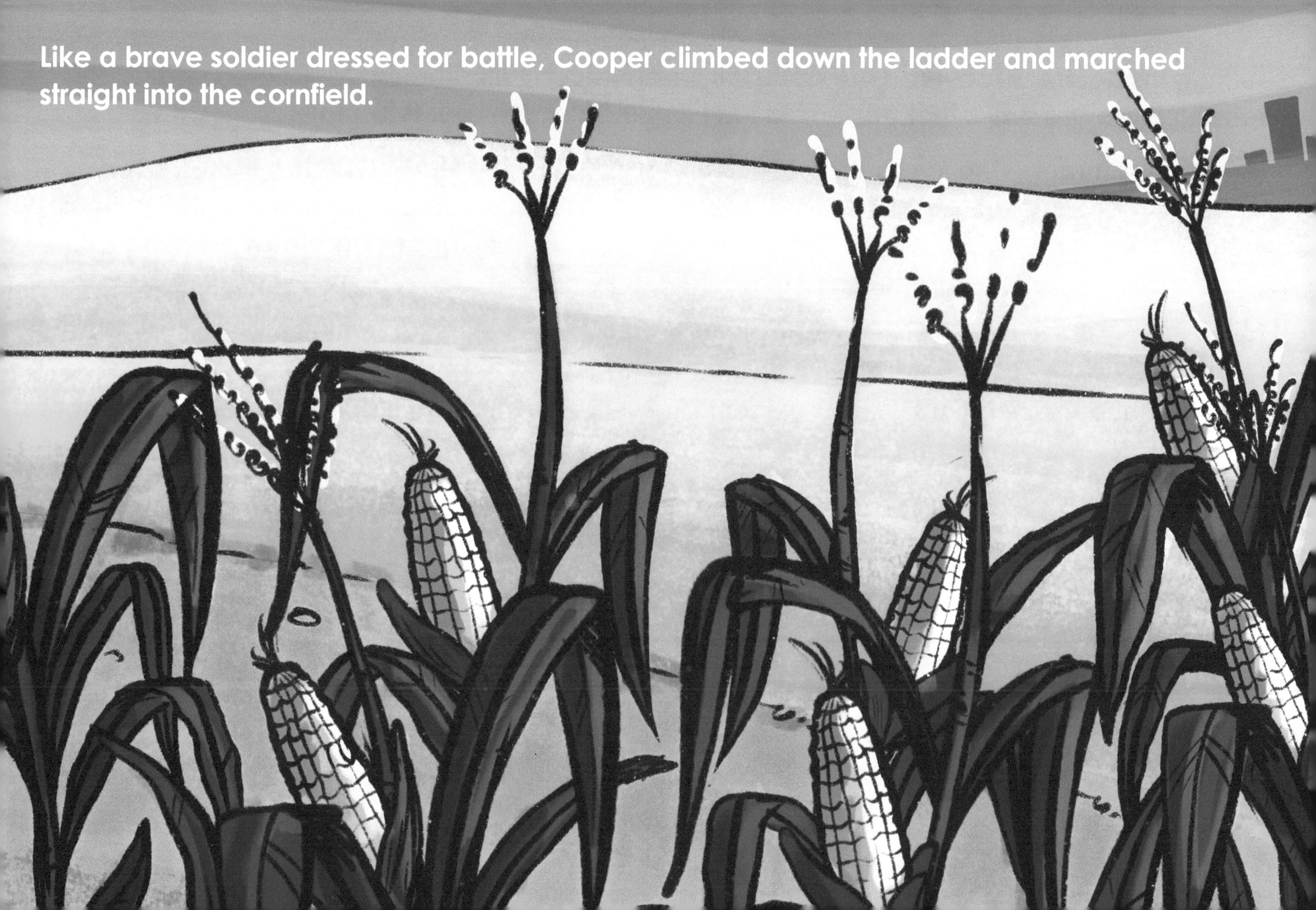

Lurking inside, he discovered the cornstalks were much taller than he expected. Standing among the giant stalks that appeared to reach the sky, Cooper felt small.

He roamed through the stalks, listening to the curious noises. Startled birds fluttered away, and grasshoppers and other insects made loud chatterings. The cornfield was a lively place in the dark. His mother was right, though. It was muddy. But Cooper liked how the mud squished between his bare toes.

He explored the corn rows, but it was much darker in the cornfield than in his backyard. As his bravery wore off, he wondered if his mother had been right again. Maybe he should not have gone to the cornfield, with or without shoes. Perhaps he wasn't fearless after all. Cooper stood still. He looked down at his muddy toes and couldn't believe what he saw.

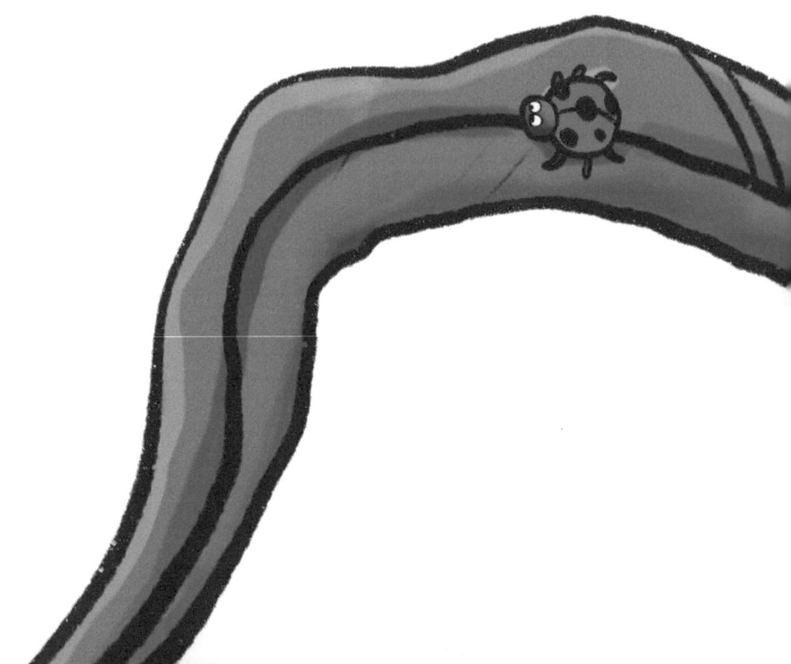

It was something so remarkable that he never expected to find. He peered through his binoculars to get a closer look. Cooper could not believe his eyes.

Cooper found a dinosaur! Not just any dinosaur... a giant, fantastic blue dinosaur with yellow stripes! Cooper was thrilled. He was looking for adventure, and he found it!

Cooper studied the creepy reptile. It was ugly. It amazed Cooper that he was not one bit frightened. No, he was feeling brave.

He sat beside the creature and pondered all the neat things he could do with a pet dinosaur. As much as he loved Spongy, a dinosaur would be much more exciting to hang out with. This dinosaur could become his new thinking companion. But would a dinosaur fit inside the treehouse?

And while he was sure they would have lots of fun taking walks together, would his new pet scare the neighbors?

He imagined inviting his friends over to play with his dinosaur. Climbing on a dinosaur would be like going up a mountain. And what a terrific ride a kid could have on a dinosaur that was tall enough to reach the sky. Oh, what a boy could do with his very own dinosaur.... IF his mother would let him keep it.

Cooper headed home to share the discovery with his mother, but it was too late. She stood at the cornfield's edge with her hands on her hips—a classic sign that he was in serious trouble. She didn't have to say a word.

Cooper's heart was thumping, his curls dripped with sweat, his knees were knocking, and his feet clumped in the mud. Now he had a much bigger reason to be brave. Cooper was in BIG trouble!

"Mom… my! There's a DIN… O… SAUR in the corn… field!" He said, trying to catch his breath.

"Oh, really… there's a dinosaur in the cornfield?" his mother said, folding her arms. She didn't believe in dinosaurs, especially not in the cornfield. She was sure this was just another one of Cooper's many games.

"No, really. There is!" Cooper said. "Come and see!"

"Okay, Cooper, let's check out your big dinosaur."

Cooper was excited! He clutched his mother's hand and led her into the cornfield. "Mommy, you'll see. It's the most incredible dinosaur… EVER!"

They tiptoed around the large stalks, his mother trying to avoid the mud while Cooper happily danced through it.

Cooper handed his mother the mud-splattered binoculars. “Look!”

“Goodness. What a surprise! Wait here.” His mother turned back toward the house. “I know just what you need,” she yelled as she ran.

What kind of mother would leave her little boy with a

dinosaur in the dark? Cooper thought.

Within minutes, she came back and handed him a small box. "Let's put your dinosaur inside. After all, if he's going to be part of the family," she winked, "he needs a bed."

Cooper's eyes grew as big as saucers, and he flashed a wide, toothy grin. He had the coolest mom. Not every mother knew that dinosaurs made terrific pets.

Looking down at the dinosaur, he realized his pet wasn't that big. Cooper was sure this beast would not scare his neighbors one tiny bit. Beaming with pride, he picked up his pal, gently placed it in the box, and closed the lid.

Walking back home with his mother, Cooper knew that his daring journey to the cornfield was worth the trip. He learned he loved scrunching his toes in mud. He even discovered that his mother knew a little about having fun.

Best of all, he found out that being brave is a choice.

He also learned that following rules is a choice, and he promised to ask permission the next time he wanted to go exploring.

About the Author

Diana LéGere is a journalist and inspirational writer with over 20 years of experience in the writing and publishing industry.

She authored four books in the Christian Living genre, including two memoir journals, Ripples: A Memoir of Reflection and He Spoke: A Memoir of Grace, and a gratitude journal, Celebrations of Praise: 365 Ways to Fill Each Day with Meaningful Moments. Not one to shy away from challenges, Diana has also published a southern cookbook and has another cookbook in the works. Her latest venture is writing and publishing children's books.

This is her first children's book, and she hopes it will be fun for young readers. Diana looks forward to writing more children's books as she seeks to inspire a new generation with wholesome and delightful messages. A creative and fun-loving person, Diana has a heart for children's spontaneity and curiosity, allowing them to embrace silly moments. She hopes to create books with light-hearted stories that inspire laughter and joy.

When not working on a book project, you'll find Diana curiously wandering about town with a notepad, jotting seemingly ordinary incidents that she hopes to one day turn into a picture book. Her creative space is adorned with plants, notepads, piles of pens, and a cherished framed rooster picture hand-drawn by her grandson, Sawyer. She loves all things creative and laughing out loud, especially when they involve the shenanigans of her little Chihuahua, Pablo.

CPSIA information can be obtained
at www.ICGtesting.com
Printed in the USA
LVHW010020070123
736631LV00003B/131